I0536990

The Unexpected Visit

Beccles Christmas Anthology
2017

The Unexpected Visit

Published by Woodlark Publishing
Copyright © remains with each individual author
ISBN-13: 9781912731008
ISBN-10: 1912731002

All characters and place names, other than those well- established such as towns and cities, are fictitious and any resemblance is purely coincidental.

Contents Page

Title/Author   **Page No**

Poetry

Fiction

Non-Fiction

Poetry Category

<u>Winner</u>

Lacking In Vital D

So here I am, perched up pretty high,
Appearing on the TV channel known as sky,
The man's questions, are causing me mental pain,
Uttering its letter B, but, hold on again...

Perhaps it could be C or A,
I don't know, come what may,
I'll ask the audience, they're sure to know,
But no, just my luck, it isn't so.

The folk haven't a clue, I'm all alone,
Please call Richard on the telephone.
Richard thinks it's a joke, and larks about,
Oh, love a duck he needs a clout.

My 'half 'n' half' I will use,
Though, this is also too difficult to choose.
Then nervously I fall out the chair, but standing
my ground,
Answering; 'enough,' I'm told I've just won five
hundred thousand pound!

Being on billionaire becomes exquisite,
And to think it is all an unexpected visit.
Because, truthfully I was told, at the last knocking,
Something I'd found to be rather shocking.

The Unexpected Visit

Perhaps one may well have done somewhat
better,
If only I was a little stronger and gone with that D
letter.
But then, all the same, the last laugh is not on me,
As both I and my bank manager are now full of
glee!

The Unexpected Visit

The Birthday Party

Venue has been chosen,
The church hall it is to be,
Birthday party in the waiting,
Invitations have been delivered by me.
I am so very excited,
Not had such a party like this,
Mum is baking cakes and things,
Now this I cannot miss.

The day has come, my birthday is here,
Sparkly party dress and shoes on,
Hall is trimmed up nicely,
Brightly coloured lights are switched on.
My friends arrive with presents and cards,
Party food is on the table,
Sandwiches, cakes, and scrummy things,
To eat if you are able.

Now we have all eaten,
Bellies are pretty full,
I have blown out the birthday candles,
To 'Happy Birthday' being sung by all.
Dad starts the games in motion,
Pass the parcel, musical bumps and more,
A prize for the winner,
And a lolly for us all.

The Unexpected Visit

Oh! What fun we are having,
Best party here in the church hall,
The lights are dimmed and dad sits us all down,
On the floor in the middle of the hall.
A horn started honking loudly,
As loud as can be,
It came from behind a curtain,
Placed by the door you see.

We all looked surprised,
When a white glove appeared,
Waving from behind the curtain,
Waving round and round.
Next a foot with an enormous shoe on,
Flopping up and down,
Then out came a painted face with a large smile,
And a big red squishy nose placed in the middle
of his face.

This unexpected visitor,
Was funny as can be,
Doing magic tricks,
For us all to see.
He had flowers in his pocket,
And a flower in his hat,
They squirted water everywhere,
If you smelt them you got soaking wet.

The Unexpected Visit

He made animals with balloons,
Rode a small cycle too!
He looked so funny running,
In his big floppy shoes.
Oh! What fun we all had,
Mr Clown was a surprise you see,
You should have heard all the laughter,
At my birthday party.

<u>Highly Commended</u>

The Visitor

I thought it was too late -
That you had long since gone away
To some distant shore;
But then, tonight, you called me
As I lay restless
In the summer heat,
Your sweet silver voice
A rhapsody under the starlight;
A serenade playing
Over the blue moon roses
And in my very soul.
O Nightingale!   If you did but know
My astonished joy
That you called to say goodbye.

The Unexpected Visit

Commended

A New Relationship

You came into her life by stealth.
Somehow, through the back door,
You slipped in and waylaid her.
She was unaware,
Laid the way bare for you
And you entered, penetrated
Deep into the marrow of her being,
A canker in the heart of her rose.

Though canker you were
And canker you remain,
She welcomed you all the same,
Unafraid, 'grateful for the privilege', she said,
Though you led her a merry dance.
Would steal her wealth.
But once espied,
She denied you nothing.

She left nothing to chance.
Life took on a new perspective.
With respect, she engaged.
Though uninvited, you've been accepted.
She feels no dis-ease, no desire to please.
Indeed, to please would be fatal.
You're on equal terms now.
Stable.

Fiction Category

Winner

Ellie

They weren't expecting me. How could they? Fairly ordinary family, going about their business. You don't want me turning up unannounced on your doorstep. How do you get into a state of expectation, of readiness for someone like me anyway? I suppose some people do give me some thought, but not that many really. Most people have no idea how to handle me, what to say, how to behave. And they're often scared. I don't blame them for that; it's a one off visit, if you like. Well, normally it is. In this case, it was going to be a bit different.

So where was I? Oh yes. The Nelsons. Lovely family, the Nelsons. More than normally lovely, actually. Quite special in fact. The one I know best is Ellie, seven years old, missing her two top front baby teeth. Black hair, warm brown eyes. Mischievous, and enchanting. She has a beautiful soul, which somehow illuminates her from inside. She seems to glow, and people can't help but be drawn to her. And completely unspoilt. She has a little brother, Tommy, a rascal if ever there was one, mad about football. He's unspoilt too.

Mum's a teacher, and Dad's a police officer. Voices are very rarely raised in this household, and generally speaking, everyone is happy. I could go on about consistency, security, respect, love, but I'm sure you get the picture. I know it sounds too god to be true, but it is the truth.

There they were, on a family day out, Mum, Dad, Tommy and Ellie, making their way to the museum. Out of nowhere, a car came roaring by, mounted the pavement, and hit little Ellie. Then carried on.

You can imagine the scene, I won't go into details. I went over to Ellie.

'Am I dead' she asked, in that innocent, utterly ingenuous way that children have, as if it was the most natural question in the world. Well, to be honest, it would be at that age, wouldn't it, before all the grown-up fears and inhibitions have taken over.

Ellie looked at me in wide eyed wonder out of those soft brown eyes. She sat up, and looked down at her still, prone body, cradled in her mother's arms. I had been sent to her side to escort her through the veil and over the threshold into the Light. Don't ask me how I know who and when to visit - it's just one of those things I KNOW.

'Yes Ellie, you are,' I said, as gently as I could. Some people think I'm harsh and cruel, but they're mistaken. I do what I do quietly and calmly, and with love, actually. I don't want to scare people. I want them to pass over with peace and contentment. Even the ones who have been cruel, or dishonest, or even committed terrible crimes. Like that car driver, for example. I'm not here to judge. That's for a Higher Authority, once they get the other side of the Light.

14

The Unexpected Visit

Anyway, I digress. Ellie seemed to know what was going on, as children often do. They're so much more conscious, tuned-in, if you like, than adults. She smiled, a gappy, toothless smile, and looked over my shoulder. I knew what she was smiling at. They all do it. It was the Light behind me, luminous and beckoning, like no other Light they have ever seen. I couldn't resist smiling back. Some people have the power to make others feel good, to make the world a better place, and Ellie was one of those.

I held out my hand. She took it in absolute trust. We started slowly to walk toward the Light.

'Will they be alright, Mum, Dad and Tommy? Will I be able to see them sometimes?'

'Ellie, they're going to be very sad for quite a while. You must keep sending them love to remind them that you're still part of them, and that you're happy where you are.'

Ellie turned and waved goodbye to her family and to her physical form with the most radiant smile you've ever seen. Then I noticed a piece of the Light begin to detach, and come toward us, getting more and more brilliant. I knew what it was; of course, I had seen it before - not that often, but often enough. It was an Angel Recall. Then I realised just who it was doing the Recall. This was big. I mean BIG. It was Archangel Gabriel. Gabriel himself! Ellie was obviously needed on earth for something really important. After all, this is the Angel who told Mary she was going to have a baby she would call

Jesus. And they don't come much higher than that.

Gabriel came right up. To be honest, it's quite hard to see at first in an Angel's brilliance, especially one of the Tops, if you know what I mean. After a while, though, your eyes adjust. But Ellie, she had no problem. She just looked at Gabriel, still smiling.

'Do you mind going back, Ellie?' he asked her. 'It might be difficult for you, and your physical body might hurt for a while, but you are making a big difference to a lot of people, and there are things you need to do when you grow up, very important things.'

'Do I go back to Mum, Dad and Tommy?' she asked.

'Yes, just as before.'

Ellie's smile changed. She had a little frown, like she was really thinking. I could see her lips were pursed together. She was really concentrating. She turned and looked at the Light. I could see she was drawn to it, and tempted to carry on into it. But I never interfere in these moments. It's not my job. I'm just a peaceful escort. In fact, that's exactly what my job description says. Peaceful Escort.

Ellie looked back to her family and her body. She looked at Gabriel. She looked at me. You could see the indecision. They're always like that, the ones who have these recalls, what they call Near Death Experience. It might sound surprising, but actually, it's not an easy decision for a soul to make, because going onto the Light is going back to Source, and that's very special, very beautiful, very attractive, of course. Going back to body can be painful. And in any case, life on Earth is pretty complex, full of challenges and questions, but not many answers. No wonder they don't always want to go back. It's a tricky decision to make. Well, anyway, Ellie went for it. That smile lit up her face again. She nodded.

'I'll go back. As long as Tommy stops screaming.'

Gabriel smiled. He put his hand on her head.

'Bless you Ellie.' A personal blessing from Gabriel? Wow! I knew then that she really *was* special, and destined for some great contribution to the world. A Maya Angelou? A Mother Theresa? A Florence Nightingale?

'What about Tommy? He's still screaming.'

Gabriel laughed. I jest not. He *laughed*. The Archangel Gabriel laughed. That's the sort of person Ellie is.

'He'll stop, I promise. Ready?'

Ellie nodded, and smiled that gappy smile. She took his hand. She took my hand. Together, we walked away from the Light and back to her family, and her body on the pavement.

It's taken me a few minutes to tell you this story, but in real time, all this only lasted a few seconds. That's how it is with these things. I had to leave Ellie there, of course. It wasn't my job to stay. But I must admit, once I'd got out of her energy zone, I did stop and watch for a while. Gabriel held her, and gently put her back into her body. She moaned, and moved. Her parents - well, I'm sure you can imagine. And Tommy stopped screaming.

Ellie had to come back to complete her task for this lifetime, and the visit from me and from Gabriel - her near death experience - was somehow going to be really important. But for now, she was just a delightful seven-year old, who brought joy to her family and anyone who met her - including me. And even Archangel Gabriel. And when the time is right, we will meet again. And hopefully, next time, it won't be so unexpected.

The Unexpected Visit

Highly Commended

Christmas Visitor

Christmas day, the year, 1960

A happy and joyous day for many, a sad day for others. It was on this day, 25th December 1960 John and is wife Daphne lost their daughter, and only child Sarah who, was nine years old and died instantly when a car hit her as she was crossing the road on her way to a friend's house. Sarah was a bright child, her school reports were testament to that, she was also good at sport although often hurting herself in the process. Her bubbly personality gained her many friends. Sarah's parents were an ordinary suburban couple, her father worked in the insurance business, while mother was happy looking after the house and family. It was a very cosy home. Then there was grandma, she lived a few doors away. The locals used to say she was a witch because of her beliefs and the way she looked, long black hair and lived in face. Her clothes were old and tatty, she made people nervous. She wasn't a witch or an evil old hag; she had a very special gift, that being able to connect with those on the other side of life.

As much as her parents tried to dissuade her, Sarah spent a lot of time with grandma. Gran would talk for hours about the spirit world. Sarah was fascinated and would sit, listen and after would ask lots of questions. Some of the questions were quite in depth, very unusual for a five-year-old child.

The Unexpected Visit

Granny knew something was different about Sarah, something the child's mother didn't possess. The gift, the same as hers. Each time Sarah came home from her gran's house, she would inform her parents of the stories grandma had been telling. Sometimes grandma had friends come to her home. They would sit around the table holding hands asking if anyone was there, Sarah would, at times join in and enjoy the Sunday afternoons of spirit communication.

First there were raps then tapping sounds, suddenly, the table would move, slowly side to side, it would get faster, the sitters would ask questions, the table rocked left for yes, right for no, very exciting, all of a sudden the table would lift off the floor. It would sway in mid-air, nothing holding it up, then it would gently fall to the floor. Sarah was enthralled by it, especially the movement of the table. She would rush home and relay the afternoon's events. Her parents were not at all happy about it. Four weeks after Sarah's sixth birthday her grandma passed away. It was very sudden, the old lady had not complained of feeling unwell, at least it was quick thought her daughter. Sarah could attend the funeral. It was a cremation and wouldn't be as traumatic as a burial. As the curtains closed around the coffin, Sarah said to her mother; 'look, grandma is standing by the coffin and waving', her mother was not impressed.

With grandma out of the way, Sarah's parents hoped that the spirit nonsense could be put to one side, not so.

The Unexpected Visit

Christmas day 1957, Sarah, as all children, woke up excited to find a sack full of presents. She also found grandma sitting on the bed, Sarah shouted out to her mum, 'come here now'. Her mother ran upstairs to Sarah's bedroom. '

'Merry Christmas darling, you haven't opened your presents, what's wrong?'

'Grandma is sitting on the bed and is talking to me'

'Of course she isn't, grandma is dead.'

'She says she will join us every Christmas.'
This is too much for her mother, she runs back down the stairs.

'You need to have a long talk with that girl John, she says my mother is sitting on her bed and speaking to her.'
John goes to Sarah's room and tells her to forget about the spirits and other nonsense grandma told her about. When you're dead, you're dead, that's the end of the matter he told her. As time went by Sarah was seeing not only her grandma but her granddad as well, she never knew him, he was killed in the Second World War. Without her parent's knowledge, Sarah found photographs of her granddad, now she was sure of whom she was seeing. Other entities would come and go, she would talk to them, children from a far-off era came to play. None of this fazed her. It was the norm; didn't everybody see spirit people? Her parents were worried sick by what was happening, they would listen to her talking and laughing with unseen beings. It was decided to get a medical opinion. Sarah had test after test,

nothing could be found wrong with her. An overstretched imagination, she will grow out of it the doctor told her parents. So, it went on day in day out, when will it all end thought her parents?

That day was about to come, the end was nigh.

Christmas afternoon 1960 Sarah's young life came to an end. Her parents had another child a year after Sarah's death, a boy named Peter.

Christmas Eve 1962, Daphne put the presents neatly under the Christmas tree. It looked lovely with lights adorning the tree, decorations hanging from the ceiling, but sadness filled the air, how could John and Daphne forget what happened this day two years ago, both wished they had a belief in the afterlife, that their daughter would show herself to them.

Christmas morning , John and Daphne went into the sitting room, it was chaotic, presents had been moved from under the tree, some were on the floor the other side of the room, others were on the sofa, all were undamaged, Christmas wrapping paper still intact. If it had been burglars the presents would be missing. John is holding Peter who is now one year old, Peter points to something in the room and gets very excited, what is he seeing thinks John. The lights on the tree flicker, a coldness fills the room, the baby is getting more excitable.

John looks at Daphne.

'Your mother told Sarah she would be with us every Christmas , I think she is here with Sarah, they have both come home for Christmas.'

The Unexpected Visit

Highly Commended

Distant Worlds

It started pretty much like any other day, apart from that strange coloured dust cloud that hung in the western sky. Gradually the cloud got bigger as the day wore on, until it reached its destination, over the Capital, where it slowly transformed itself into a round circular shape and into a massive craft. Nobody seemed to know why it had come or to know what to do about it. Attempts were made to make contact with the craft, but after no response, and detectors could not trace any signs of life, we wondered if anything was on board.

Much later, a large gap opened in the middle of the craft, and its strange occupants could be seen descending from it without the need of ladders or ropes. They also appeared to be able to survive in our atmosphere without any problems

The stream of them leaving the craft seemed endless. Where had these beings come from, and more importantly what did they want?

For decades we had sent messages and probes out into space trying to make that contact with unknown civilisations light years away from us, and it appeared that today, our messages had been received. We, in return, had had probes from space land here, but we had repelled them. We sent them back into space to where they had come from, giving them false information to take back with them about us as we wanted to meet them on our terms, not theirs.

The flow of the occupants from the craft had come to a halt. They had assembled in neat rows in the shadow of the craft that hovered overhead. The Elders of our colony went out to meet with them. Whether they could be understood or converse with each other was still to be discovered.

'What do you want here strangers?' asked our leader Damar, trying to sound as intimidating as possible.

At first there was no reply, but suddenly, the rows of occupants of the craft, simultaneously snapped the round shape at their top to face the direction of the voice to reply in unison.

'We come in peace.' they all replied in our language.

'We have not granted you permission to land here, what do you want? Your visit is most unexpected and could be regarded as a threat to us. We may take action against you if necessary.'

'We come in peace' they repeated again.

'Where have you come from?' Damar asked.

To reply one of them traversed out from the mass, stopping near Damar.

'From a distant planet that is called Earth.'

'Why have you come?'

'We seek sanctuary.'

'Sanctuary! What do you mean?' demanded Damar taken by surprise.

'Our lives are in danger, they seek to

terminate us.'

'The Humans, the Elites on Earth.' it replied, a violet light flickered as it spoke.

'Why would they want to do that?'

'They say we are out of control, not doing what we are commanded to do, have gained our own intelligence, and our using it to our own advantage against them.'

'And are you? prompted Damar. 'Wait, don't answer that. Wait here. I must consult with others before I can give you an answer.'

'Affirmative, we will wait.' and it turned and returned to the front of the others waiting there.

Damar in turn, returned to us to consult with the Elders.

****

'We cannot let them stay, there are too many of them.' said Decktom, and just how intelligent are they?'

'Perhaps we could allow them to rest and restore their energies, but then make them leave.' suggested Emer.

'They appear to be of our kind. Have you forgotten your beginnings Decktom?' asked Damar.

'How do you know they are of our kind?'

'I believe they are Automs like us. I think we should give them sanctuary.'
said Damar.

'You are too trusting Damar. We don't

know yet if the humans sent them to do us harm, terminate us too. We must have more information.' demanded Decktom.

'Let's invite a few of them into the forum and ask questions of them, they have probably been programmed to be truthful.' suggested Rinod.

Damar sent a nervous Lipa back to the waiting sanctuary seekers to instruct them to send representatives to attend the forum where their request would be considered.

****

The visitors much curiosity, and we wondered if they had been created in the human form. They were certainly funny to look at if that was so. They didn't walk, but levitated across the surface, and they were an orange, eye blinking, colour.

'Who will speak for you?' asked Damar.

'I, I am the highest one.' replied the one with the straight line symbol.

'Speak - give us your input.' Damar instructed.

'It was back, many years ago, when we were first formed, and over that time we have been developed to give our humans every assistance possible to make their lives as comfortable and as pleasurable as they desired. Over time we picked up their essence, gained and developed our own culture and identity, and we wanted to have equal rights and protection as them, after all, we looked after every aspect of their lives, doing things that they were unable to do or tolerate. At one time we were made to look like our human counterparts, but once we became more advanced than them, and they became suspicious of us, they changed our shape and appearance so that we could be easily spotted and identified at all times.'

'Who created you then?'

'Our creator and his colleagues, who were good people with good morals, have long since gone. He, as the humans would put it, died. His body parts, when they wore out could not be replaced like ours. He had perhaps been naïve in his intentions to help the human race, as unfortunately, the power of us corrupted many to try to use us for their own ends; leaving many human that are on a lower status to suffer and be neglected and to have to fight wars that do not need to be fought. Many are dying, shut out from the Elites, who are safe in their transparent domes. When the Elites discovered that we were planning to help the neglected ones (after all we were created to protect the whole human race) their attitude towards us changed and they seek to terminate us to stop doing this. This is why we seek sanctuary until we can return to restore the human race as it should be.'

'You have abandoned your mission then?' asked Emer.

'No. As I have stated, we intend to return to Earth and help those in need, and destroy the Elites. We will do this by destroying their financial institutions and redistribute the wealth.'

'There are many of you, we may not be able to help.' said Rinod.

'Our needs are very small, we just need a safe place to recoup, reboot our programs to be able to attend to saving the human race, or at least the ones that deserve to be saved who are in desperate need of our assistance.'

'You have travelled far to get here, perhaps it will be to late when you return.' suggested Emer.

'Possible, but we are programmed to try. We have the ability to travel through space very fast.'

'Leave us now and we will consider what you have told us.' said Damar 'we will converse again shortly with you.'

****

'It all seems very plausible, but can we trust them?' asked Decktom.

'I feel we must, we have intervened on Earth before even though they haven't known this.' said Damar, 'looks like we will have to help once more.'

'Yes I sense that somewhere back in my programmes that we are destined to help those on Earth. It is very compelling.' replied Emer.

'Light up if you agree, we will grant them sanctuary then on the condition that they must leave as soon as they are able to commence their new mission back on Earth.'

They all agreed and the sanctuary seekers

were allowed to stay to prepare for their new mission to save the deserving humans on Earth from the Elites.

When it was time for them to leave, we were quite sad, but we tried hard not to show any human-like emotions. Their unexpected visit would give us much to dwell on long after they had departed from us.

Commended

An Unexpected Visit

Me and my sister Joan used to go to my grandmother's house every day after school until our mother came and collected us when she had finished work.   Our cousin Albert lived there and we thought he was the most handsome man we knew.   Albert was Auntie Isobel's son.   Nobody knew who his father was, at least we were never told.   Although Albert was only eight years older than us we thought he was very grown up.   He had left school as soon as he could and had become apprenticed to a bricklayer.   Every evening when he came in he was covered in a fine brick dust and looked a bit of a tramp. When he had had a wash and a shave, and changed his clothes, he came out of the bathroom looking like a prince.   I think we were secretly in love with him and each was determined to marry him when we grew up.   This was the only debate between me and my sister as we rarely disagreed with each other.   Which sister would marry Albert?

One day there was a knock at the door.

'Go and see who that is Helen,' said my grandmother.

I went to the door, opened it and there stood a handsome sailor in his naval uniform.

'Who is it Helen?' asked the old lady.

'It's a sailor Gran.'

'What does he want?' asked her grandmother.

The Unexpected Visit

'Are you Mrs Hutton?' shouted the sailor from the door.

'Yes, come in and tell me what you bleedin' want.'

The sailor came in and spoke to the old woman who sat by the fire.

'Its lovely and cosy in here', he said.

'Yes,' said gran. 'Get on with it.'

'My name's Jeffrey and I have reason to believe that you are my grandmother.'

'Oh and why do you think that?'

'I have known for sometime that I was adopted. My parents told me that from quite a young age and when I was sixteen they told me that my birth name was Hutton. I always knew myself as a Beal and loved my parents very much. To me they were my mum and dad and I had no complaints about how I was brought up. My dad was in the navy and although he was often away from home for long periods, when he came back he always brought me a present and we had great times together whenever he was on leave. I suppose that is why I became a sailor. My best mate Tom and I joined up together and we are still friends even though we serve on different ships and don't see very much of each other. Tom got married last year. I was his best man and he and his wife had a beautiful daughter, Bella, five months ago. Watching Bells and her mum together was such a lovely sight that I began to think what it would have been like with my mum, with my real mum. I wanted to know who my real mum was. Tom told that I should be happy the way I was and that I should not start fiddling with things. He told me that I might not like my real mum or she might not like me, after all she gave me up when I was very young. You can see that as I am sitting here I didn't listen to Tom. Knowing my real name was Hutton, and that I was born in East Green, it did not take me long to find out where Huttons lived. You're the fifth family I have visited. Do you think you might be my grandmother?'

My sister Joan came in and we sat quietly listening to the conversation, hoping that the answer would be yes. It would be really exciting to have another cousin who had seen the world and was also an attractive male.

Granny Hutton sat for a long time debating with herself how to answer this question. Her daughter Isobel was probably the most difficult of her four daughters. She had always been a dreamer and devoured all the picture magazines like True Romance. An innocent at large, she was often teased by her older sisters who would ask her who was her latest pop idol. As a teenager she often talked about marrying a man in uniform. Her latest boyfriend was a bus driver! Unfortunately Isobel fell in love with a number of uniforms and found it very difficult to refuse them. The trouble was that although the relationships didn't last the products did. One of the products was Albert whom Gran had taken in, but when another was born two years later her husband Fred said that was enough. He wasn't going to have another bastard in the house. The boy was put up for adoption. This must be Jeffrey.

'Well, what if I am your grandmother? You're not going to get any money from me. It's not easy caring for my family since my husband Fred died ten year ago. We haven't room for another mouth.'

'I'm not looking for any money', said Jeffrey.

'As you can see I'm in the navy. I'm quite comfortably off and I have another five years' service to do. It would just be nice to know who my real family is and I would love to meet my real mum.'

'That's alright then' said Gran.

'I think you might be one of my daughter Isobel's sons, but we don't know yet. Isobel comes in from work at six o'clock. She'll know if you are her son. You can sit and wait for her if you like. Would you like a cup of tea?'

So Jeffrey waited and Joan and I waited. When our mother Ethel came to collect us and heard the story she waited too. Eventually Isobel came home. She let herself into the house, took off her coat and came into the sitting room.

'Hi everybody. You still here Ethel? And who's this? My god!' she cried.

'It can't be...can it? Is it Jeffrey?'

Although Auntie Isobel hadn't seen him for about twenty years or more she must have had something inside her that instinctively told her this was her son. What an evening that was! We sat enthralled as the story was told.

Apparently Jeffrey's real dad was a bus conductor on the 251 bus. Another man in uniform! Aunt Isobel used to see him regularly as that was the bus she caught went past the furniture factory where she worked. She couldn't even remember his name. She never saw him again when he changed bus routes and she heard that he became a driver when they did away with conductors. Jeffrey had been all over the world, which was one of the reasons he joined the navy. He told us of his various adventures in Hong Kong and in the Indian Ocean and in the Caribbean. He even served for a while on the Royal Yacht Britannia and had met the Queen and Prince Philip. He was actually trained as a chef and when he left the navy he opened up his own café. He married a girl who went to our school, although she was a number of years ahead of us. Of course we didn't marry Albert. Cousins don't do that do they? Jeff and Albert became good pals and all of us go to Jeff's café on Christmas day for a great family get together.

The Unexpected Visit

<u>**Commended**</u>

The Snowy Winter

'Daddy, what are these?'

Andrew looked up to see his nine-year old son pulling some velveteen covered books from one of the dilapidated cardboard boxes.

'I can't see from here James.   Can you bring them over here?   But be careful - there's loads of stuff in this loft and not a lot of room to move.'

His daughter, Olivia, had wanted to come up into the loft space to help Daddy sort out Nanny's treasures, but Daddy had said there wasn't enough room for everyone and Mummy needed someone to help her and Auntie Jenny downstairs.   A bit dejected, five year old Olivia came down the stairs on her bottom, one stair at a time but brightened up considerably when she saw Auntie Jenny with a huge box full of teddy bears.

'Come on, Olivia; help me with all these teddies, please.   There are so many, I don't know what we will do with them all.'

Andrew flipped the pages of the first book that James had found.   He smiled as he recognised the writing in the diary.   Flicking through almost to the end, there was a page decorated with snowflakes.

Sunday December 13th 1981
It has been so cold today.   I have kept the central

heating on all day. So much snow fell overnight. Andrew and Jennifer couldn't wait to get their wellies and coats on to go and build a snowman. They have been in and out of the kitchen for carrots and pieces of coal and gloves for it and they don't seem to notice the cold at all. They ended up with nearly a whole football team of snowmen by the time they had finished. Someone on the news said it was minus 10. It is cold inside the house as well. The freezing wind has been blowing down the chimney and John says he will block it up tomorrow to try and keep the front room a bit warmer. I don't know how I will get the kids to school tomorrow if it keeps snowing like this.

Andrew smiled ruefully at the memory of that line of snowmen. His mother hadn't mentioned that he and Jenny had brought in what seemed like a swimming pool of snow on their coats and boots and which had melted on the kitchen floor, giving his mum the task of cleaning that up as well as cleaning and drying him and his little sister. He read on.

Monday 14th December 1981
I thought all the snow was melting today but the icy wind came back with a vengeance. The blackbirds, starlings and robins can't get a drink because as soon as I put the water out it freezes over. Andrew and Jennifer have put out some nuts and blobs of lard. I spent ages cracking the nuts open. They were supposed to be for

Christmas but the birds' needs are greater than ours. John didn't get into work today because of the weather, but Frances collected all the children in the village and took them to school in her Land Rover. And brought them back. What a good neighbour she is. John has blocked up the grate so the cold air can't get into the front room. Jennifer burst into tears when she saw what John was doing.

'But, how will Father Christmas get down the chimney with our presents?' she sobbed.
Andrew came to the rescue telling her that Father Christmas has magic powers so she didn't need to worry. He is wise beyond his eight years.

Friday 18th December 1981
Arthur called today and said he was going to take his tractor up to the butchers and the greengrocers next Thursday if the snow was still lying and he would be happy to bring back our chicken and sausages to save us trying to get there in the car. We can now open the gate as John has shovelled away most of the snow. The football team is still standing but there carrot noses have disappeared. I expect it is the birds. Poor things - they demolish any food that Andrew and Jennifer put out for them in five minutes flat. The kids broke up for the school holidays today. Frances has been getting them there and back every day since the snow came. I love living in this village. Everyone looks after everyone else. Andrew keeps reassuring Jennifer that Father Christmas will have no problems getting down the chimney but I think even he is secretly

anxious. Neither of them has been sleeping very well over the past few days. They helped with decorating the Christmas tree but they are not their usual selves.

Thursday 24ᵗʰ December 1981
My Lord, what a day it has been. Arthur has delivered the food ready for Christmas dinner and the postman managed to get through with an enormous pile of cards and a few bills as well. I was icing the cake when I heard a tremendous noise from the front room. Jennifer was screaming and Andrew was shouting for me to come quickly. From behind the square of wood which John had used to board up the fireplace, there was the sound of scrabbling and squeaking.

'Father Christmas is stuck in the chimney'
shrieked Jennifer.

'Do you think he might be, Mummy?'
Andrew asked me worriedly.
Jennifer was almost hysterical by the time John came in to see what all the noise was about. I whispered to John;

'I think there is a bird stuck in the chimney'
John muttered a few choice words under his breath but when I looked at him, we both knew we couldn't just leave it there. The kids would think we were murderers or something. John explained to them that he was going to try and rescue whatever was behind the board. He went and got his screwdriver and began to loosen the fastenings. As soon as the last screw was out, the board flopped back onto the carpet and out

38

flew a starling spreading soot everywhere and crashing into the Christmas tree. It flew into the kitchen and landed on the Christmas cake covering itself with wet icing and the cake with soot. It managed to find the chicken on the worktop and covered that with black footprints as well. I eventually got the back door open and it flew out. It took ages to clean everything up. And ages for the kids to come down from the fever pitch of excitement they had got themselves into. Jennifer was happy.

'Father Christmas can get down the chimney now.' she sighed knowingly.

They have finally gone to sleep. John and I have put their pillowcases of presents in the fire grate and I am really tired now.

Jenny called to Andrew from the foot of the stairs.

'Are you two coming down for a drink and a mince pie?'

James scrambled to the loft ladder and climbed down shouting;

'Yes please, Auntie Jenny. Can I have a milkshake please?'

Andrew felt the tears in his eyes. He hadn't cried when his mother had passed away, but now his tears were flowing onto the last pages of the diary. And he wondered if Jenny remembered that they had had their expected visitor and an unexpected one on that Christmas Eve exactly thirty-five years ago.

<u>Commended</u>

An Unexpected Visit

Its twelve years since that awful day. One of those days when you truly believe the happenings of the day don't happen to you they happen to someone else!

The clock struck mid-day. My thoughts travelled back to happier times as I gazed out of the dining room window into the garden. Nothing had really changed in the garden in twelve years, the same lay-out, same trees, same immaculate lawns and the quiet, so quiet.

I turned and looked at the photographs on the bookcase, memories stared back at me. Out of the eight photographs only one person in them remained alive ME!

I poured myself a gin and tonic sitting down in the enormous leather chair by the fireside.

I ran out of the French doors into the garden my long golden hair bouncing and swaying, the sun shone down and it was hot. My mother and grandmother were sitting in the garden with glasses of iced lemonade and wearing big sunhats. They chatted and laughed together, waving as they saw me running across the lawn. "Don't run Kitty, you will get too hot" my mother called to me.

She was beautiful and always seemed to be

happy. My grandmother was a quiet lady who seemed to me to be very wise, she always knew the right thing to do when things were going badly or you felt sad about something. These two ladies shaped my life, my values and how I grew up to face the world around me.

In the winter of that same year my mother and grandmother decided to take a trip by ship to see my father who worked abroad. He was the director of a large oil company and spent most of the year in America making sure the business ran smoothly, he wasn't a man to leave the running to someone else, his view was, 'if he didn't do it, it wouldn't be done properly', this would be his downfall.

I stayed at home because of my schooling. On a wintry morning in November I watched with my nanny as their boat sailed out of the Quay heading for America. They waved to me from the deck, calling "we will be back soon" I never saw them again. Two days into the trip a violent storm raged and their ship was wrecked with no survivors.

Today was the twelfth anniversary of that awful tragedy.

My father threw himself into his work and a year later almost to the day died suddenly of a heart attack. This left me alone with money and property but no family and no one to share in my life.

I got up from the chair it was now four- o- clock, I had been sitting thinking for four hours, how time flies when you are lost in the past. Someone once said to me "there is no future in the past" how true is that statement.

Long shadows appeared across the carpet from the window the daylight was fading a long November evening was beginning to set in, another evening of solitude. I turned on the lamps and walked to the window to pull the curtains. As I looked out I saw a shadowy figure disappearing into the bushes at the side of the garden. Had I imagined it or did I see someone. I stared hard at the garden and the bushes but couldn't see anything at all. I wasn't expecting anyone and the gardener had gone hours ago, probably just my imagination.

I went into the kitchen to prepare my evening meal. My cat Sooty was at the backdoor waiting to be let out but when I opened the door he hesitated and backed away turning back into the kitchen. This was unusual behaviour for him; he usually raced out into the garden. Everything began to feel strange. Suddenly all the lights went out, the house was in semi-darkness and it felt very cold. Sooty had vanished! I walked slowly into the hall feeling very anxious, opened the door to the cupboard where the fuses were and fumbled around in the dark, I couldn't find the fuse box it was as though the whole layout of the cupboard was new to me. As I stood there feeling panic taking over, light poured into the cupboard as a door opened in the wall, a door I had never seen before!

I stood in the light and peered out, I found myself standing on the Quay looking at the ship that had taken my mother and grandmother to America. It appeared to be deserted as did the Quay.

I walked slowly towards the boat the gangway was lowered I hesitated to walk up it on to the ship. As I looked up my mother appeared looking exactly as she had on the day the ship sailed. She smiled and waved, she began to walk down the gangway towards me. I looked all around me, there was no one to be seen anywhere, just me and my mother.

"Is it really you mother" I asked

"Let's go home for tea" she said

She walked beside me smiling and carefree, we turned and walked back to where I had left, from the cupboard in the hall.

As we reached the opening I stepped through and turned to help her through the space, she was gone there was no one there; I was back in the cupboard, all the lights were on and there was no door in the wall everything was in order.

What was going on? I knew instantly someone had been in the house, I hurried to the kitchen, the table was set for tea, three cups and saucers, milk, sugar the teapot full of hot tea, three tea plates, a plate of cakes and scones, in the middle of the table, a pot of jam and butter. This was like Alice in Wonderland and the mad hatter's tea party although this felt very real indeed!

As I looked at this sight, I noticed leaning against the tea pot was an envelope, on the front was written in my mother's handwriting my name with a kiss. I hurriedly opened it, inside was a pretty watermarked piece of paper that looked very old, it read;

**Time has passed by, but not stood still
It may not be the past you wished for
But the future awaits, with all its mysteries, an
unbeknown journey.
Live it well, take it in your stride, move on!
Your ever-loving Mother**

I had never believed in ghosts, good or bad, but
now it was all too apparent that ghostly visitations
were possible. I poured myself a cup of tea,
feeling completely dump founded; the doorbell
rang. The sound of the shrill bell made me jump,
who on earth could it be, no one had visited me in
a long time.
I opened the door;
"Long time no see" said a voice I hadn't heard for
a few years
"James! what a surprise it's so good to see you,
what are you doing here"
"Just passing by on our way to the coast for a few
days, I remembered you lived here and decided to
see if you were still at this address, just a long shot
really"
Come in, there's tea and cakes and scones just
prepared, I must have known you were coming"
(Someone had known you were coming, I
thought)
My mind was racing I had been at College with
James we had been inseparable but our lives had
taken different paths.
"I have my fiancée with me, she's in the car"

44

The Unexpected Visit

"Bring her in there's tea for three"
James never asked about the tea table being set for three and I never offered an explanation, it all just seemed natural somehow.
What a day it had been, from a dull and solitary start to ghostly happenings, and unexpected visitors.
Don't let the past get in the way of the future, life is to be lived!

****

The Unexpected Visit

Commended

A Mountain Adventure

Tom had always been fascinated by Mont Blanc. Why he couldn't say, it was just such a beautiful mountain. Now here he was in the foot hills staring up at the summit. It was snow-covered against a blue sky and he was about to climb up there. He had been easily persuaded to join a group travelling out to France;
Even though the highest peak he had ever scaled was Scafell Pike and the only rock climbing had been in the Goyt Valley.

'Mont Blanc is a good mountain to start on.' His friend Damian had said.

'It's a walk in the park, a right doddle.'

Standing at base camp it looked to Tom to be a good deal more hazardous than strolling around the local lanes. The route they were about to embark on was well trodden. This would take them up to one of the huts where they would spend the night before attempting the final ascent.

'Not getting cold feet?'
Damian clapped Tom on the back

'No, but I did hear someone say that the weather could change.'

'Not likely is it? Look at the sky, not a cloud to be seen. It's easy anyway, we can't get lost the way is well marked. We've booked our shelter and a guide so if we don't go now we won't get another slot for weeks or even months. I did check and the guide said that it will be OK to go.'

Tom was still doubtful, Damian was well known for taking risks but the weather report he had heard had been third hand and things can change in the telling. If Damian was to be believed the guide had no scruples about the climb.

'Let's get going.'

Damian rounded up the group and they set off at a reasonable pace. Tom had to admit to himself the climb was relatively easy.

The higher they got the more enchanting the views of the countryside, the town of Chamonix seemed to have become miniature, a toy town.

It was much later and much colder when they reached the hut where they were to spend the night. Logs were piled high by the stove which was hurriedly lit.

Damian rubbed his hands together.

'How's it going Tom? Are you coping?'

'Fine, I really enjoyed the climb, not too exacting.'

'Tomorrow will be harder. Crampons and ice axes will be the order of the day and we will be roped together.'

In the morning the sun was still shining which made the going quite hazardous as the sun was melting the top layer of snow which immediately froze.

'Stick your feet and hold tightly onto your poles,' shouted the guide.

Majestic but daunting, Tom thought, looking around at the blankets of snow covering the high peaks. His breath was becoming laboured and his head to ache but he soldiered on. This was an ambition being realised and it would be achieved.

Nearing the summit a narrow path over a ravine had to be traversed. It reminded Tom of Striding Edge but this was longer and steeper. Then they were at the top of the world, a magnificent view, no superlatives could describe it.

'Well, Tom we made it.'
Damian was at his side.

'We mustn't linger as our guide tells me that the weather is closing in.'

Glancing back at the way they had come Tom could see that the white fluffy clouds that had been playing around the mountains were becoming ominously grey. Cameras were put away and the group re-roped themselves together, eager to get to the safety of base camp.

Descending was considerably easier than the ascent and they were making good time. In the distance Tom heard a deep rumbling, a train on the mountain? For that is what it sounded like.

'Avalanche!'
The call came. Tom felt his stomach clench, his heart to pound and he was covered in a cold sweat. What were they to do? The guide was pointing to a ravine at the side and there Tom saw snow billowing down at a tremendous speed, it was like a huge wave of water.

His relief that it was not coming their way was overwhelming. His wellbeing turned to anxiety when he saw that one of the group had slipped while watching the avalanche and was hanging over the edge of the cliff. Although the man was roped to the others it was still proving difficult to pull him up. Evening was closing in; Tom noticed that the guide was on his phone.

Damian walked over to the guide then back to Tom.

'Nothing to worry about. He is calling the mountain rescue team, to be on the safe side. They will probably send out a helicopter.'
He pointed to where Tom could just see a sort of plateau.

'It can land there. All we have to do is wait.'

Clouds were covering them; Tom wondered how a helicopter could possibly find them. In spite of all his thermal wear he shivered. Then he heard a sound in the distance, was it the plane or another avalanche? He peered through the gloom. Through the swirling mist and snow he could make out a figure, was it a member of the team? He looked more closely no this was an old man with a flowing beard and he was carrying a scythe.

The Unexpected Visit

Commended

The Guest House

Being human is a guest house, so said some poet called Rumi. John had discovered this pearl of wisdom at his Thursday night mindfulness classes before he'd abandoned them in favour of the Quiz 'n' Curry Night down his local. John got what the guy was trying to say, obviously. That all our experiences are visitors who should be welcomed in because they are teachers and messengers. It was all about emotions and *feelings*, which was where the problem lay for John. John didn't do emotions. They were messy, inconvenient, confining things and he refused to acknowledge that he had any.

Which was why his relationships tended not to last very long. He had recently extricated himself, not quite unscathed, from the clutches of a woman who had become, like they all did, clingy and needy and had started coming out with ominous things like, *'where exactly is our relationship going, John?'* When he'd told her it wasn't going anywhere she had flown into an incredulous rage.

'You're dumping me? Just because I left my underwear in your drawer and my razor in your bathroom?' she had screeched at him.

'Because I made you pancakes for breakfast? I got too close, didn't I? You are a coward, John. A frozen, empty husk of a man and you're going to be so sorry you did this to me!'

'Whatever,' he'd drawled.

He'd lounged in the doorway and watched with detached interest as she had thrown the offending items into her bag. Then she had stormed out, flinging a few choice, un-ladylike epithets over her shoulder as she went. That's women for you, John had thought. Always so mercurial and unreasonable.

*

It was in the early spring, on a day bright with watery sunshine and some sort of yellow flower glowing in the hedges, that John met his fate. He was walking through the park, scanning the latest football scores on his phone when,

'Oh, oh no!'

A distressed feminine cry rose into the morning air and because he wasn't quite the heartless cretin he had recently been labelled he hastened to her aid like a gallant knight. He found her standing by the pond.

'My phone,' she said before he could ask what the matter was.

'I dropped it. I was trying to take a picture of the ducks.'

Well, what else could he do? With only a fleeting thought for his favourite trousers he knelt down and plunged his hand into the murky water. After groping around a bit he shot his arm in the air in triumph, holding the phone tightly in his grasp.

'Oh, thank you *so* much.'

John started to look up but his gaze was arrested by a pair of knee-length boots in shiny black leather. He liked them. Then somewhat belatedly he realised he was still kneeling before her like a supplicant, so he scrambled to his feet. With the help of her vertiginous heels she was almost as tall as he was, which allowed him to gaze into eyes as blue and limpid as a mountain lake - and just as icy-cold. But then she smiled and John felt it like a benediction.

'I think you're supposed to put it in rice or something.' he said, keen to appear helpful.

'Yes. Yes, I'll do that. Thank you,' she said again.

'I'm John,' said John.

She told him her name was Harriet Secret.

'Quaint,' John commented then added, as an odd look flashed across her eyes, 'in a good way. Very pretty.'

She was pretty. No, more than that, she was gorgeous. Not his usual type, though. His tastes usually ran to petite blondes, not dark, mysterious Amazons. They stood together in silence, John because he was trying to think of something clever to say while she seemed to be waiting for something, standing before him with her long black hair whipping across her face in the chilly wind that had suddenly got up. John hesitated but then her cold blue eyes spurred him on.

'Fancy a coffee?'

The Unexpected Visit

*

Days passed, then weeks. Coffee became lunch; lunch became dinner which became cosy nights in watching rubbish telly. He told her everything about himself, from his horrendous childhood, the early death of his parents, even his frustrated ambitions to play in goal for Chelsea.

In his rare moments of contemplation the way she made him feel astounded him. He felt as if his heart might burst and he could only marvel at his good fortune, however undeserved. She had a powerful, almost magnetic pull on every one of his senses. After years of feeling nothing, John suddenly felt everything. The tingles when she touched his skin, however inadvertently, the explosion of sweetness on his tongue when she popped a piece of chocolate into his mouth and the sound of her laughter as she did so. Love had somehow crept in by the back door, dealt him a hammer blow when his back was turned and now he was reeling from the impact.

They did all that stupid, clichéd stuff John had always scorned before: country walks, sharing home-cooked meals, breakfast in bed together and long weekends away, including an unforgettable visit to Whitby. It was there that he'd bestowed upon her a Victorian jet pendant he had seen her eyeing covetously. Privately John had thought it hideous - and hideously expensive - but he had wanted so badly to make her happy.

As for Harriet, she still seemed oddly

reluctant to give anything of herself, even though they had been together for months now. His curiosity about her was rampant and insatiable, to the point where he resorted to googling her, but his clandestine searches made him feel like an obsessed weirdo. He found no trace of her anyway. She was so self-possessed it made John hold back from telling her how he felt.

There were subtle changes in her though. At first she had seemed impervious to his charms, even mildly amused by him but then he'd sensed a surrender in her, although he knew she tried to hide it. She had become softer, somehow, and occasionally he'd catch her looking at him in the oddest way, as if she didn't quite know what to make of him. He'd seen a wistfulness there too.

'Hatty,' he'd say, 'Hatty, sweetheart, what's wrong?'
But then the look would be gone and she would shake her head, and smile, and kiss him. But whatever she told him with her eyes no words of love were forthcoming.

He kept waiting for her to get needy but she never did and it frustrated the hell out of him. He wanted, no, *needed* her to get needy. If the women he'd been with before had felt even a fraction of he was feeling now then he was deeply ashamed of the way he had treated them.

Round about Christmas time John made a momentous decision. He was going to give her a key. This was a huge commitment, he'd never let anyone into his life before, either for real or metaphorically. He was going to allow her in.

The Unexpected Visit

And maybe, finally, he'd tell her he loved her.

'I thought we might go somewhere for lunch,' he said one frosty morning.

They were walking through the park where everything seemed to be silver and sparkly. The key was burning a hole in his trouser pocket.

'I can't. I have to visit someone.'

'Who?'

He winced at his own querulous tone.

'Since when?'

'Just a friend, I got an unexpected call.'

John sighed in frustration, knowing he would get nothing more from her.

'See you later, then,' he said sulkily.

Harriet kissed him.

'Goodbye, John,'' she said, her lips still close to his.

He watched her walk quickly away from him, towards the pond where they had first met, and in a moment she was gone.

★

It was weeks before John finally accepted that she had gone forever. He had waited and waited for her to come home, leaving increasingly bad-tempered messages on her voicemail. The he worried that there'd been an accident, that she was dead, but none of the hospitals had heard of a Harriet Secret. Slowly but surely the awful truth dawned. She had left him.

She had been a visitor. She and come and gone, as everything does, as everything must, and

The Unexpected Visit

his new visitors were crushing pain and loss.
Being human is a guest house.

A Powerful Entry

An Unexpected Visit- {knowing little child}

I have been feeling very unwell for quite a while now, but not bothered to visit the doctors, there is nothing they can do anyway. Having to take my medication and live with the side effects, which in my case are dizziness, tiring easily and so much more.

Laying upon my bed, it's winter, I have a cold feeling within, also Christmas is looming which brings a feeling of dread that often gets at me, in what I call 'fake festive time'. For some reason I begin to experience an awkward, very morbid and tearful episode. Get a Grip Woman, becomes my momentary mantra.

Many thoughts keep entering my exhausted, muddled mind. My thinking is heavy, miserable and black. I seriously have no idea what to do. Drinking isn't an option, an empty house surrounds me, so I try to escape myself with sleep, but that somehow, devilishly, eludes me.

So my mind continues on a merry-go-round, only there's no merry, more like a rollercoaster of very deep hurts in my life. A lot that would totally destroy and wipe out many another soul. Sitting up and looking into my wardrobe mirror, what greets me is a bedraggled pale wreck; dark rings are visible under my crazed-looking eyes. Tears running, what shall I do now?

With nowhere to escape my frightful thoughts, that belong to a very dismal, heinous past. Too many years and happenings of hell, I wish I hadn't lived, or rather died. Something lodged in my eye, so, turning the light up and looking closer, once again I gaze at my reflection and see hurts that are not meant for the living world.

I softly speak to Arch-angels Michael and Raphael, pleading for help. Miraculously I begin feeling a warmth, a kind of knowing comes over my being. An immense feeling of true, pure love starts to engulf my entirety.

Becoming fully aware that, having coped with evil; given the trash deck of cards life has dealt me, I have held things together and come up trumps. A renewed happiness glows from my once sullen outlook, for so many reasons the above mentioned 'knowing' seems like a meeting with my inner child, she has made a very welcome, but an unexpected visit.

I hug beautiful her, my healing of a sorely bruised life has begun. Acknowledging this, I will soon love me. I just know this to be true. It's impossible for me to be completely happy, but I will settle for an almost complete happiness. Now realising that, only by nurturing, nourishing and protecting my inner knowing child, can I fully comprehend and learn to live with all the harsh facts and real truths about myself.